D1571363

Read & Feel™
PUBLISHING

ISBN 979-8-9856727-0-1

Published by Read & Feel Publishing
Brooklyn, New York
(646) 980-0471

ifyourbestfriend.com
readandfeel.us

Printed in China

IF YOUR
BEST FRIEND
IS A
Mermaid

If your best friend is a Mermaid
That friendship is forever.

And there are so many amazing things
That you will do together.

When a mermaid becomes your best friend
There's something you can do.
You get to choose your mermaid's name,

A name that sounds
Magical
To you.

An important thing to know
Whenever you feel fear.

With mermaid magic you get to swim
Without any **DIVING GEAR!**

As you swim down to the ocean depths,
The water starts getting dark.

But something now alarms you:
Look out you see a **SHARK!**

Luckily, the shark is the mermaid's friend.
He's just a toothy grinner.

You swim away with great relief.
You thought you would be **DINNER!**

You help your best friend do her chores.
It's really quite a feat.

You get to use a GIANT comb,
To keep the seaweed neat!

Will you get squished by massive whales?
Things are looking dire.

No not at all. You get to sing
With an underwater CHOIR!

You see a row of mighty clams,
And when they open wide.

They show you all the beautiful *Pearls*
That they have made inside.

You help to feed the dolphins,
Stroking them with care.

They take you swimming DOLPHIN-STYLE,
And you fly through the air!

It's time to go eat at the castle.
You hope lunch has many courses.

And to get there,
You ride in a *golden* carriage,
Pulled by six seahorses!

If you spill a drink when you're at home,
It causes a MESSY commotion.

But not when you're drinking underwater.
It just washes away in the ocean.

The carriage *ZOOMS* through the water,
You're having such a blast.

And because your best friend is a princess,
The fish bow as you swish past.

You've had the best time, but now you're exhausted.
The time has come to go home.

But when your best friend is a mermaid,
You don't have to travel ALONE!

As you close your eyes
And go to sleep.

The mermaid sings a **SONG.**

Then she magically transforms into a doll,
So she can stay with you all night long.

Find more best friends
With the continuing Book Series

IF YOUR
BEST FRIEND
IS A
Unicorn

From the New York Times Bestselling Author
Adam Wallace
Illustrated by **Alice Pescarin**